Dear Reader,

This story is all about my first time on a plane. It was fantastic!

It describes all the things that we saw at the airport as well as our flight.

I felt that I was particularly helpful in this adventure. I don't know why the other passengers were laughing.

We hope you like our story and, most importantly, we hope that you find it useful if you are going on a plane too.

Yours truly,
Munks

# For Mum, who loves flying!

Text and Illustrations Copyright © 2003 Brooke House Publications Limited
Created by Brooke House Publications Limited, Worcester

**First published in Great Britain in 2003**
by Brooke House Publications Limited

www.brookehousepublications.com

ISBN 0-9543556-2-8

Printed and bound in Great Britain by Ebenezer Baylis & Son Ltd

# MUNKS GOES ON AN AEROPLANE

by
Mary Allan

Illustrated by Roger Hancox

# CHAPTER ONE

Munks woke up full of excitement. He jumped out of bed, ran to the window and looked up at the sky. He had been dreaming about aeroplanes.

Today he would be going on holiday and he'd be flying on a plane for the first time.

He quickly got dressed and ran to fetch his case. "I'd better pack," he said. "I've got so much to do. Let me see," he muttered, "I'll need swimming trunks and water-wings in case I go in the sea. I'll need T-shirts and I'll need my spade for making sand castles."

Munks knew that he needed his passport because he was going to another country. He took it out of a drawer and looked at the photograph inside.

He remembered having the picture taken.

There had been a stool to sit on and a curtain so that no one could see into the photo-booth.

The camera flashed when it took the picture and it made Munks jump so that he ended up looking rather surprised.

Then, because he thought it had finished, he was getting off the stool just as the flash went off for a second time, so Munks scrambled back onto the seat just as the flash went off again.

By the final flash he was looking very fed up.

His two best friends Corby and Humphrey had waited for him outside. They giggled when they saw the pictures. It was only the promise of a jam tart that had cheered Munks up again.

Now he looked at the pile of things on his bed and wondered how he was going to get it all in the case. He didn't want to leave anything behind.

"Hello Munks," Corby's cheery face appeared around the door. "I thought you may need a hand this morning."

"Hello Corby, perfect timing," said Munks, "would you help me to close this?"

His friend looked at the heap of clothes and toys and shook his head. "You won't be able to close it like that," he said.

Corby took everything back out of Munks' case and folded it neatly for him.

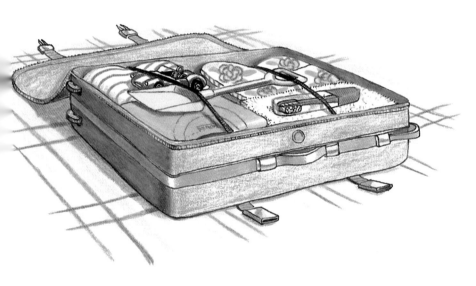

Finally everything was packed properly. "Thanks," said Munks.

Just then there was a knock on the door and their friend Humphrey arrived. "Good morning everyone."

"I've just finished packing," said Munks, hopping from one foot to the other.

"Jolly good," said Humphrey. He turned to Corby. "Have you packed yet?"

"Oh yes," said Corby putting a big paw up to his special hat.

"Well in that case I think we've got time for a snack," said Humphrey.

Munks trotted off to the kitchen.

"Munks is looking forward to his holiday," said Corby, "but I'm a bit nervous. I know it's silly but I don't know if I will like flying."

Humphrey frowned. "That's not silly," he said. "It's normal to feel afraid sometimes. Lots of people feel differently about different things. I find that it helps if you talk about your fears."

"Well I've never been on a plane," said Corby, "so I don't know what it will be like."

"That's easy," said Munks running back into the room. "Humphrey can tell us all about it."

The friends ate their favourite jam tarts as they listened to Humphrey.

Corby felt a lot happier after Humphrey had finished.

Munks was bursting with excitement. "Can we go now?" he asked.

"Not yet," said Humphrey. "We've got a bit of time to wait."

"We could help you to tidy your house," said Corby looking around him. Munks had managed to get red jam everywhere.

"Thanks," said Munks. "You do that while I go and check my packing again."

# CHAPTER TWO

Later that day the three friends were finally standing in the airport.

They joined a queue at the check-in desk.

"Good afternoon," said the check-in assistant. "Where are you going today?"

"On holiday," shouted Munks.

Humphrey handed over the tickets and passports.

She looked at Munks' suitcase. "That will have to go in the hold," she said.

"What's a hold?" asked Munks.

"The hold is a big space under the plane. It's like a car boot," explained Humphrey.

"Ok," Munks said. "But be careful because there are some very important things in there."

"We'll look after it," she smiled. "Are you taking anything else?"

"Just my small bag," replied Humphrey.

"That's ok," she said, "that's small enough for you to carry. Here are your boarding cards. You will need to go to gate C."

Munks, Corby and Humphrey set off to join a line of people.

"Now what's happening?" asked Munks.

"These are special metal detectors," explained Humphrey. "All the passengers walk under the arch and if they are carrying anything metal the machine 'beeps'".

Munks walked through very slowly but nothing happened so he wanted to go through again.

Corby guided him away before he got into trouble.

Suddenly Munks shouted, "Humphrey, your bag's been eaten up! Don't worry I'll get it back."

He jumped on a conveyor belt and tried to scramble through a tunnel after the bag but Corby just managed to grab one of his legs and pull him out.

"It's ok Munks," said Humphrey. "All the bags have to go through this x-ray machine. Here's my bag now."

Corby, Humphrey and Munks went to sit by a window to watch the planes landing and taking-off.

After a while their flight was called.

"Passengers on flight G5T6 now go to Gate C."

"Quick," said Munks. "They might go without us".

There were lots of people getting on the plane. A stewardess checked their boarding cards and told them that they would be sitting in seats 5A, 5B and 5C.

Munks lead the way down the aircraft aisle to row 5 and he sat by the window but to make it fair they agreed to swap around through the journey.

Humphrey helped him to fasten his seatbelt.

"Do the pilots wear these too?" Munks asked.

"Yes," said Humphrey. "Everyone wears a seat belt."

Munks watched everything that was happening.

"What's that noise?" asked Corby.

"It's just the engine starting up. Aeroplanes need engines to fly just like a car needs an engine to make it drive," explained Humphrey.

"Now we must be quiet for the next bit," he said. "There is always a short safety message before a plane takes-off. Watch and listen carefully."

Munks paid attention to the crew then the airplane started to move forward.

"You'll like the take-off," said Humphrey, "the plane has to go very fast."

Munks held the arms of his seat as the aircraft started to go faster and faster and faster.

Everything whizzed past the window then suddenly Munks felt the aircraft lift up.

"That was great!" he said. "Now what happens?"

"Well you might hear a noise when the pilot brings the wheels up. Then you just sit back and enjoy the flight," said Humphrey.

"I hope he remembers to put the wheels back down," said Corby, who had closed his eyes for the take-off.

# CHAPTER THREE

When the plane had been in the air for a while the cabin crew started to serve food and drinks.

"Will they have jam tarts?" Munks asked Humphrey.

"You'll just have to wait and see.  When it's your turn one of the cabin crew will ask you what you would like."

Munks wanted to explore.

"What does this do?" he asked, looking up at a button above his seat.

"You won't need to touch that," said Humphrey. "That's for people who need to call the crew."

Munks reached up and pressed it.

A steward came over to him. "Can I help?"

"May I go to the toilet?" Munks whispered.

Corby and Humphrey looked at Munks. "You don't need to press the button for that," they said.

"That's all right," replied the steward.

Corby and Humphrey stood up to let Munks out of his seat.

He was gone for rather a long time.

They were just starting to wonder where he was when they heard some passengers starting to laugh.

Then they saw him coming back down the aisle, pushing a food trolley.

A steward ran after him. "Could I have that back please?"

"I was just trying to help," said Munks. "There are rather a lot of passengers to serve."

"Perhaps I should go and help the pilot
instead," said Munks looking towards the front
of the plane.

"I think it might be a good idea if you stop
getting up and down," said Humphrey.

Munks climbed into the middle seat.

"I know what we can do," said Corby. He
reached up to his special hat and produced
some playing cards.

Time went by quickly as the friends played
games, read books and ate their snacks.

Suddenly Munks started to shake his head. "My ears are blocked up," he said.

"That happens sometimes," explained Humphrey. "It's all to do with the air inside the plane. Try yawning or swallowing to clear them again."

Munks yawned. "They're still blocked," he said.

"Here you are," said Corby pulling a handkerchief from under his hat. "Try gently blowing your nose."

Munks blew his nose noisily then 'POP' his ears cleared.

An air stewardess appeared next to them. "We'll be landing soon. Please fasten your seatbelts."

"Ok," the three friends replied together.

"What's that noise?" asked Corby as a clunking sound came from underneath the plane.

"That's just the Captain putting the wheels down for landing," answered Humphrey.

Munks stuck his head under the seat.

"Perhaps I should go down there and give him a hand."

"He's not actually under the plane," said Humphrey.

Munks leant across Corby who had his eyes closed again. "We're nearly there!" he shouted, a bit too loudly.

Then, with a small bump, the airplane landed.

"Listen to the loud noise when the pilot slows the plane down," said Humphrey.

"Wow!" gasped Munks.

The Captain made an announcement. "Ladies and Gentlemen please stay in your seats until the plane has stopped."

Munks, Humphrey and Corby waited for the seat belt sign to go off. "Right," said Humphrey, "have we got everything?"

"I have," said Munks.

"So have I," said Corby, but before anyone had a chance to stand up Munks was climbing over Humphrey and making his way towards the door.

When the passengers were off the plane they had to have their passports checked. The man checking them took a long time looking at Munks' picture.

Then Munks was off again.  He had spotted his case with a lot of other bags.

"I can see my blue suitcase!" he shouted. "Corby, please will you help me?"
"Certainly," replied Corby making his way to his friend's side.  "Here we go," he said lifting the case up and placing it on the floor.
"Shall I get a trolley?"  He turned to where Munks had been standing.

"No need," Munks called over his shoulder. "I'm sure you can manage," and with that he was running off again, heading for the exit.

"Keep up with him," said Humphrey.

Munks turned around. "Come on!" he shouted to his friends. "I'm hungry and that suitcase has got........."

"........your jam tarts in it?" finished his friends.

Munks grinned. "How did you guess?"

Corby and Humphrey started to laugh at his cheeky face then all three friends laughed and laughed and laughed.

THE END